FRIENDSHIP CLUB

Strawberry Shortcake

Halloween Hideout

By Megan E. Bryant
Illustrated by Laura Thomas

Grosset & Dunlap

AMERICAN GREETINGS

American Greetings and rose logo is a trademark of AGC, Inc.

GROSSET & DUNLAP
Published by the Penguin Group
Penguin Group (USA) Inc., 375 Hudson Street, New York, New York 10014, U.S.A.
Penguin Group (Canada), 90 Eglinton Avenue East, Suite 700, Toronto, Ontario,
Canada M4P 2Y3 (a division of Pearson Penguin Canada Inc.)
Penguin Books Ltd, 80 Strand, London WC2R 0RL, England
Penguin Ireland, 25 St Stephen's Green, Dublin 2, Ireland
(a division of Penguin Books Ltd)
Penguin Group (Australia), 250 Camberwell Road, Camberwell, Victoria 3124,
Australia (a division of Pearson Australia Group Pty Ltd)
Penguin Books India Pvt Ltd, 11 Community Centre, Panchsheel Park,
New Delhi - 110 017, India
Penguin Group (NZ), 67 Apollo Drive, Mairangi Bay, Auckland 1311,
New Zealand (a division of Pearson New Zealand Ltd.)
Penguin Books (South Africa) (Pty) Ltd, 24 Sturdee Avenue, Rosebank,
Johannesburg 2196, South Africa
Penguin Books Ltd, Registered Offices:
80 Strand, London WC2R 0RL, England

Library of Congress Cataloging-in-Publication Data

Bryant, Megan E.
Halloween Hideout / by Megan E. Bryant ; illustrated by Laura Thomas.
p. cm. - (Friendship Club)
"Strawberry Shortcake."
ISBN 978-0-448-44558-8 (pbk.)
I. Thomas, Laura (Laura Dianna) II. Title.
PZ7.B8398Hal 2007
[Fic]-dc22
2007000984
10 9 8 7 6 5 4 3 2 1

Chapter 1

Ding!

"The cupcakes are ready!" Strawberry Shortcake exclaimed as the timer rang. Her house was filled with the sweet scent of pumpkin and cinnamon as she carefully removed a tray of cupcakes from the oven. "Mmm," Strawberry said. "I can't wait to share these cupcakes with my friends!"

It wouldn't be long before Strawberry would be able to do just that. The Friendship

Club was having an important meeting that afternoon. Halloween was just two weeks away, and it was time to start getting ready!

Strawberry frosted the cupcakes, then put on her coat and left for the meeting. The trees along the Berry Trail were covered in red and gold leaves. Just a few weeks ago, it had still felt like summer in Strawberryland. But now, though the sun was shining brightly, there was a chill in the air.

Strawberry walked into the clubhouse. "Hello!" she called. "Anyone here?"

"Hey, Strawberry!" a boy's voice called. It was her friend Huckleberry Pie. "It's just me so far."

"Hi! Hi!" Blueberry Muffin ran into the room breathlessly, followed by Orange Blossom. "Are we late?"

"Nope," replied Strawberry. "Have a cupcake!"

Soon Ginger Snap and Angel Cake arrived. Strawberry smiled as she handed out cupcakes to her friends. Ever since the friends had started the Friendship Club, Strawberryland was full of excitement. Strawberry loved spending time with her berry best friends—and the Friendship Club gave them the perfect reason to hang out more than ever!

"This cupcake is delicious," Ginger said. "I love it!"

"Me, too. Hey, can we start the meeting now?" Angel asked. "We have *so* much to do!"

"I know! I can't believe Halloween is in only two weeks!" replied Strawberry. "This is going to be the berry best Halloween ever. Has anybody picked out a costume yet?"

The kids were silent.

"I don't know *what* I want to be!" Orange finally said.

"Neither do I," added Ginger.

"I have an idea," Blueberry said. "I'll bring my dress-up clothes to the clubhouse. You can borrow anything you want!"

"That's so nice of you, Blueberry!" Strawberry said.

"I'll bring my art supplies so we can make decorations for our houses," added Angel.

"We can also bake Halloween treats here!" said Orange.

"The clubhouse will become Halloween Headquarters!" Strawberry said. "Who wants to continue this meeting tomorrow—with all of our supplies?"

"Me!" chorused her friends.

"Great. Let's meet here

4

at noon," Strawberry continued. "Don't forget to bring your supplies so we can start getting ready for Halloween!"

The kids put on their coats and walked outside. The autumn breeze had turned into a brisk wind, and dark clouds covered the sky. Strawberry shivered. "I guess we're getting a storm tonight."

"Tonight? I think you mean *now*!" Huck yelled as rain began to fall. "See you later, girls!" He hopped on his skateboard and zoomed off to Huckleberry Briar.

"We'd better hurry," Strawberry said.

The girls raced down the Berry Trail, but by the time they reached Strawberryland, they were soaked.

"Come inside!" Strawberry yelled over the wind. "The storm is getting worse!" She led her friends into her warm, cozy house and slammed the door against the storm.

"I'm f-f-freezing!" Angel Cake said, her teeth chattering.

"Me, too!" exclaimed Ginger.

"Hang on, everybody—I'll get some dry clothes," Strawberry replied. Soon all the girls had changed into sweatshirts and sweatpants, and Strawberry was warming up a pot of apple cider.

"Mmm, this is delicious," Orange said, sighing. "Thanks, Strawberry."

"This storm doesn't look like it's going to stop anytime soon. You guys should stay for a sleepover!" Strawberry said. "It's too dark and rainy to walk home alone." The rest of the girls nodded excitedly.

"The storm reminds me of a scary story I

know," Ginger said. "Want to hear it?"

"Ooh, yes!" exclaimed Blueberry.

"Let's turn out the lights," Ginger suggested. "And I'll need a flashlight."

"You got it!" Strawberry replied. She took a flashlight out of a drawer and handed it to Ginger, then turned off the overhead lights.

Ginger held the flashlight under her chin. The light made spooky shadows on her face.

"On dark and stormy nights, just like  this one," Ginger began, "a horrible, mean old witch wanders around Strawberryland. You can see her when the moon is full and lightning shoots across the sky. She

whispers at windows and taps on doors."

Ginger stopped talking and knocked softly on the floor. The girls all jumped in surprise, then giggled nervously.

"It sounds just . . . like . . . that," Ginger continued. "So you must always lock your doors and windows so the witch can't get into your house! And if she finds you, you may never . . . be seen . . . again!"

"Wh-why? What does the witch do?" Orange asked in a shaky voice.

"No one knows," Ginger replied in a voice barely louder than a whisper. The girls leaned closer to hear. "Maybe she turns you into a nasty witch. Maybe she makes you her servant for all eternity. Maybe she just makes you . . . disappear!"

A loud knock echoed through the room. Everyone jumped.

"Who did that?" Ginger asked urgently. "Who knocked?"

"It wasn't you?" asked Blueberry.

"Not that time! Oh, Strawberry, I hope you locked the door!" Ginger exclaimed.

"I—I *think* I did," Strawberry said. "But now I'm not sure!"

"I'd better go check," Ginger said grimly. "I hope the witch isn't already inside!" She walked toward the door, taking the flashlight with her.

The girls were silent as they sat in the dark, listening to the pounding rain and howling wind.

"That story was creepy," Angel finally said. "Even if I don't believe in witches."

"Oh, you don't?" a voice shrieked behind

Angel. "GOTCHA!"

Angel screamed as a pair of hands grabbed her shoulders.

"Help! Help!" Angel cried.

Strawberry scrambled to turn on the lights. Ginger was standing behind Angel, laughing.

"Ginger! Was that all part of the story?" Strawberry asked breathlessly. "You really scared me!"

"I haven't been this freaked out in a *long* time," added Blueberry. "Good job! I love scary stories!"

But Angel didn't like Ginger's scary story or prank at all. Tears of anger and fear ran down her cheeks. "How—how could you do that?" she asked. "I thought you were the witch and that I was going to disappear forever!"

"Aw, Angel, it was only a story," Ginger said with a laugh.

"Not when you sneak around in the dark and grab someone!" Angel continued. "I hate being scared like that. How would you like it if somebody did that to you?"

Ginger stopped laughing. "Wow, Angel, I'm sorry. I didn't mean to scare you so badly. I won't ever do that again, okay?"

Angel took a deep breath and then sighed. "Okay. Thank you, Ginger," she said. "Your story started out okay. It was just the last part that went too far."

Ginger put her arm around Angel. "I totally understand. And don't worry—I would protect you from any mean old witches that tried to get you, anyway!"

"Hey, who's hungry?" Strawberry asked. "Now that Angel and Ginger have finished making up, I'm ready for dinner—and guess what we can make? Grilled bat sandwiches and bloodsucker's soup!"

"Ew! Sounds like a good dinner for a vampire!" exclaimed Orange.

"But it sounds like a disgusting dinner for girls!" Blueberry said, wrinkling her nose.

Strawberry's eyes twinkled. "Not when the 'grilled bats' are actually grilled cheese sandwiches in the shape of bats—and the 'bloodsucker's soup' is tomato soup!"

Angel laughed. "Well, in that case, I might give it a try," she said.

"Great! I think you'll really like it," replied Strawberry. "A spooky dinner during a spooky sleepover on a spooky night—the perfect way to get into the Halloween spirit!"

Chapter 2

The next morning dawned bright and sunny. The strong wind had blown the storm out of Strawberryland, leaving a brilliant blue sky behind. Strawberry awoke early to make breakfast for her friends. With sleepy eyes and messy hair, the girls gathered around the kitchen table as Strawberry placed tall stacks of pancakes before them.

"That storm was so loud! I barely got

any sleep," grumbled Angel Cake.

"Maybe you didn't get any sleep because you were whispering with Orange all night," Blueberry teased her.

"Maybe," Angel admitted. "I'm berry tired."

"Me, too," yawned Strawberry. "But I'm still excited about making Halloween plans."

"Yeah!" Orange chimed in. "I can't wait to see Blueberry's costumes!"

"I know you'll find the perfect one," Blueberry said confidently. "Hey, can anybody help me take my costumes over to the clubhouse?"

"I can help!" Ginger said.

"So can I," added Strawberry.

After breakfast, Strawberry and Ginger went to Blueberry's house while the other girls went home for their supplies. They

packed several bags and
boxes of costumes, then
went to the clubhouse.

"I guess we're the first ones here," said
Strawberry as the girls stepped inside.

"Hey, does it look brighter in here to you
guys?" asked Ginger.

"Yeah," Strawberry replied. "Maybe the
storm blew a lot of leaves off the trees so
more light is coming through."

"It's chilly, too," Blueberry said, shivering.

"I hope nobody left a window open last
night," Strawberry said. "Well, let's take
the costumes into the main room." She led
the way, but stopped short in the doorway.
Ginger and Blueberry walked into her,
spilling costumes everywhere!

"Strawberry! Watch it!" Ginger snapped.
"Look at this mess!"

"Oh no!" cried Strawberry.

"Don't worry," said Blueberry. "We can pick up the costumes in no time."

"It's not that," Strawberry gasped. "Look up there!" She pointed at a giant, jagged hole in the  roof. Rainwater dripped from the edges.

"Hi, everybody!" Angel's voice rang out. "Who's ready to start planning?"

"There isn't going to be any planning today," Ginger said darkly. "Our clubhouse got *ruined* last night!"

Angel's mouth dropped open as she entered the room. "How did that happen?"

"What's going on?" asked Orange as she walked in. Huck was right behind her.

"The storm tore a giant hole in the roof of the clubhouse," Strawberry explained.

"Oh, look at the walls. They're ruined!" Angel exclaimed. "All that hard work painting them—now they're *ruined*!"

Strawberry stepped into the room. *Squish. Squish. Squish.* "The rug is soggy and disgusting!" she reported. "It needs to be washed and dried."

"And the curtains, too," Orange added.

"What are we going to *do*?" asked Angel Cake. "Our clubhouse is a disaster! There's no way we can fix it up *and* do everything we need to get ready for Halloween!"

"Yeah—this was going to be our Halloween Headquarters," Blueberry said. "But I can't leave my costumes here now. What if it rains again and they get ruined?"

"All of our plans are ruined—not just your costumes!" Angel exclaimed. "How will we ever get ready for Halloween now?"

"Whoa," Huck interrupted. "Hold on a minute. You guys are getting really upset."

"Sorry," Strawberry said. "I think we're all tired from staying up too late last night."

"Well, lucky for *you* I got a good night's sleep," Huck teased his friends as he grabbed a flashlight from a nearby drawer. "I know just what to do. Follow me!"

Huck ran out of the clubhouse and led the girls into the Cinnamon Woods.

"Where are we going?" asked Orange.

"You'll see," Huck replied mysteriously. "Not much longer. Look over there!" He pointed at a cave tucked into a rocky hill.

"Oh, I don't want to go in there," Angel protested. "Caves are damp and dark and scary and full of bats!"

"Not this one," replied Huck. "Come on!"

Huck was right. The cave was
dry and cozy inside.

"This isn't bad at all!"
Strawberry exclaimed. "I
kind of like it here."

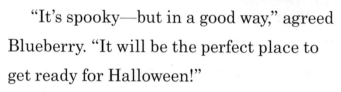

"It's spooky—but in a good way," agreed
Blueberry. "It will be the perfect place to
get ready for Halloween!"

"Told you so!" Huck said proudly. "And
fixing the clubhouse won't be that hard if
we split up the work. I can start fixing the
roof right away."

"I'll work on the roof, too," Ginger said.

"I can wash the curtains," volunteered
Orange.

"And I'll take care of the rug,"
Strawberry said. She turned to Angel.
"Angel, would you paint the walls
again?"

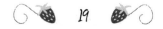

"Of course," Angel said. "But I won't start until the roof is fixed— just in case there's more rain."

"Then we'd better get to work, right, Ginger?" Huck said. "Let's go!"

"Wait a minute!" Strawberry exclaimed. "What about Halloween?"

"Strawberry's right," Blueberry said. "We can't forget about all our plans just because the clubhouse needs to be fixed."

"I have an idea," Strawberry said. "Huck and Ginger, why don't you start fixing the roof today? The rest of us will set up the cave as our temporary clubhouse—and our new Halloween Headquarters!"

"Great idea!" Blueberry said with a grin. "But maybe we should call this place the Halloween Hideout instead—because a cave makes a really excellent hideout!"

"Yeah—and we're hiding out from the clubhouse disaster," joked Angel.

"Maybe *you* are," Huck teased. "But Ginger and I are ready to work. See you later, everybody!"

Soon Huck and Ginger were on the roof of the clubhouse, inspecting the damage.

"This is a really big hole!" Ginger marveled. "It will take *forever* to fix it. What do you think happened?"

Huck shrugged. "Who knows? Maybe a tree branch did it. Maybe the wind blew some tiles off the roof."

"It *was* a bad storm," Ginger replied.

"Storms are spo-o-o-o-ky," Huck said in a funny monster voice. "But I hope we don't get a storm on Halloween. It's no fun to

trick-or-treat in the rain."

"Hey, do you have any costume ideas
yet?" asked Ginger. "I was thinking I might
be a mad scientist."

"You'd make an awesome mad scientist!"
Huck said. "Are you going to try any crazy
experiments?"

Ginger giggled. "Maybe, if there's time
to figure one out!"

"I think I want to be something scary,"
Huck replied.

"Not a skeleton, I hope," Ginger said.
"Skeletons creep me out!"

"No way!" Huck laughed. "You? Afraid
of skeletons?"

Ginger blushed. "Um, well,
yeah. That's pretty dumb, isn't
it?"

"I didn't know you were

afraid of anything," Huck said.

"One time I saw this movie on TV where a skeleton came to life. It was really scary!" Ginger shivered at the memory. "But a skeleton could never *really* come to life—right?" She reached for the box of nails.

"Well, I don't know . . ." Huck began.

Ginger's eyes grew wide. "Y-you really think that—"

"Gotcha!" Huck yelled. "No way a skeleton could come to life. Ha!"

"Very funny," Ginger replied. "I knew that. The movie was just pretend. I shouldn't be scared of something so silly."

"Exactly," Huck said. "Now hand me those nails, okay?"

Ginger grinned as she gave Huck the nails—but she still thought there was nothing scarier than a skeleton.

Chapter 3

While Ginger and Huck worked on the roof, the other kids turned the cave into a Halloween workshop. Blueberry swept dirt and dry leaves off the floor, while Strawberry hung battery-operated lanterns all over the cave. Orange and Angel brought all of Blueberry's costumes and Angel's art supplies from the clubhouse.

By the time the sun started to set, they were finished.

"It looks awesome in here!" Blueberry exclaimed. "This place is perfect for making Halloween plans."

"Speaking of plans, guess what?" Strawberry asked. "I know what I'm going to be for Halloween: a rock star!"

"Great idea! I'm going to be a vampire— that delicious 'bloodsucker's soup' you made inspired me," said Orange.

"I've had too many costume ideas!" Blueberry groaned. "I can't pick just one."

"I know exactly what I want to be," Angel said. "A fancy lady wearing a fancy dress with lots of ribbons and jewelry!"

"That's perfect, Angel," Strawberry said with a smile. "Let's meet here on Friday to make our costumes."

"Ooh, I almost forgot!" Orange suddenly

exclaimed. "My pumpkin patch is ready! Want to come over on Wednesday to pick pumpkins?"

"Abso-berry-lutely!" Strawberry replied. She walked around the cave, turning off the lanterns. "I'll call Huck and Ginger."

"Thanks, Strawberry!" Orange said as the girls left the Halloween Hideout. "See you then!"

That night, Huck was watching TV when the phone rang. "Hello?" he answered.

"Hi, it's Strawberry! Are you busy?"

"Nope," Huck replied. "I'm just watching The Monster Channel."

"Oh, I don't like The Monster Channel!" Strawberry said. "It's too creepy!"

"I know—that's why I love it!" Huck

laughed. "So what's up?"

"We finished getting the Halloween Hideout ready!" Strawberry said.

"Awesome," said Huck. "I can't wait to see it! Ginger and I fixed part of the roof—but there's still a lot of work to do."

"I know you can do it," Strawberry said. "Hey, the pumpkins that Orange grew are ripe. Can you come to Orange Blossom Acres on Wednesday to pick one out?"

"Of course I can!" Huck said. "I want the biggest, roundest pumpkin there."

"Okay—but just make sure you can carry it!" teased Strawberry. "Oh, and there's one more thing—on Friday we're going to make costumes at the Hideout."

"Sounds good. See you in the pumpkin patch, Strawberry!"

"Bye, Huck!"

Huck hung up the phone and turned back to the TV. A new movie was starting. It was about a skeleton that chased people around a small town. "Hey, I wonder if this is the movie that scared Ginger," Huck said to his pet frog, Shoofly. "It's a pretty goofy movie. I can't believe she was scared of it." A mischievous glint twinkled in Huck's eyes. "I think I know how to help Ginger not be afraid of skeletons anymore! I'm going to make a skeleton costume and when she sees me wearing it, she'll know just how silly it is to be scared of skeletons!"

"Cr-r-r-r-oak!" Shoofly replied.

"I can paint glow-in-the-dark bones on my black sweatshirt and sweatpants," Huck continued excitedly. "And make a mask! Ha! A jumping and dancing skeleton would make anyone laugh! I can't wait to surprise Ginger with the best Halloween trick ever!"

On Wednesday, when Strawberry arrived at the pumpkin patch behind Orange's tree house, she found Huck sitting on a huge pumpkin that was bigger than he was.

"Mine!" Huck said with a grin. "Told you I'd get the biggest pumpkin here."

"How long have you been sitting there?" said Strawberry, laughing. "All night?"

"Not exactly. But I did get up pretty early this morning!" Huck admitted.

"Hey, do you guys want to carve your pumpkins here?" Orange asked, joining her friends outside. Ginger, Blueberry, and Angel were with her. "I could use the pumpkin seeds for next year's patch—and for a little surprise I'm making!"

"Sounds fun," Strawberry replied. "But first I need to pick a pumpkin to carve!"

The kids split up and wandered up and down the long rows of pumpkins. Strawberry stopped to check out each pumpkin. At last, she spotted a pumpkin that looked just right. "I found one!" she yelled.

Orange ran over. "Nice work, Strawberry!" she said as she cut the pumpkin from the vine. "Here you go!"

Strawberry joined the rest of her friends, who had already finished scooping out the seeds from their pumpkins. She quickly started on her own pumpkin, scooping out the seeds and adding them to a bowl.

The members of the Friendship Club worked hard for the next hour. Finally

Strawberry looked up from her pumpkin to see how her friends were doing.

"Your pumpkins look awesome!" she exclaimed. "Blueberry, that's a spooky face. And Angel, your pumpkin looks so cheery! And Huck—are you carving a skeleton?"

Ginger looked up. "What?" she asked quickly.

"No, I didn't carve a skeleton," Huck said with a sly smile. "I carved a skull and crossbones! See? It's a pirate pumpkin!"

"Cool idea," Orange said as she picked up the big bowl of pumpkin seeds.

"Hey, where are you going?" Huck asked. "You didn't finish carving your pumpkin."

"I'll be back in a minute!" Orange said mysteriously.

"So, Ginger, do you like my pumpkin?"
Huck asked.

"Uh—yeah, I guess so," Ginger
stammered.

"I don't mind if you want to carve the
same thing on your pumpkin," Huck said.

"No thanks," Ginger said. "I, uh, don't
want a spooky jack-o'-lantern. I have my
own idea."

"Well, I like spooky things, like
monsters and ghosts and *skeletons*,"
Huck said loudly. "That's the whole
point of Halloween!"

Ginger stood up suddenly. "I'm going
home now," she announced. "I'll just finish
my pumpkin there."

"Is everything okay?" Strawberry asked.

"Oh, sure," Ginger fibbed. "I'm, ah, going
to start finding stuff for my costume. Can't

wait to show you guys on Friday! See you later!"

"Bye, Ginger!" everyone said.

A few minutes later, Orange returned to the group. "Where's Ginger?" she asked.

"She went home to work on her costume," replied Angel.

"Oh. Well, I hope you're hungry— because here's my surprise!" Orange said proudly. She held out a bowl filled with roasted pumpkin seeds.

"Awesome! I love pumpkin seeds!" exclaimed Blueberry. "Thanks, Orange!"

While the kids munched on the salty, crunchy seeds and chatted about Halloween, Strawberry wondered why Ginger had left so suddenly. It seemed like something had upset her.

But what?

Chapter 4

That night, Huck tried on his skeleton costume. "This is the best costume ever. Now I just have to make sure Ginger comes to the Halloween Hideout early." He picked up the phone to call her.

"Hello?" Ginger answered the phone.

"Ginger! It's Huck. After you left, we decided to make our costumes on Thursday instead of Friday. Okay?"

"Oh, okay," Ginger replied. "Thanks for

letting me know! What time?"

"Four o'clock," Huck said.

"Cool. Hey, do you want to fix the roof on Friday since we won't be making costumes then?"

Huck paused. He wasn't sure what to say. The Friendship Club would still be making costumes on Friday—but he couldn't let Ginger know that until after the prank! Finally he stammered, "Uh, sure. See you at the Hideout tomorrow."

Huck quickly hung up the phone to avoid any more questions. He was so excited about his prank that he had forgotten how scared Ginger really was of skeletons.

The next afternoon, Ginger put on her mad scientist costume—a white lab coat and goggles. "I'm sure Blueberry will have some things I can add to my costume," she said. "And maybe Angel will help me fix my hair so it looks all wild and funny!"

Instead of going straight to the Halloween Hideout, Ginger decided to pick up Strawberry on the way.

Ding-dong!

"Ginger! Hi! What are you doing here?" Strawberry exclaimed when she opened the door. "What's up with the doctor's coat?"

"It's my costume! I'm a mad scientist—*not* a doctor," Ginger replied. "I thought we could go to the Hideout together."

"Huh? We're meeting at the Hideout to make costumes tomorrow," Strawberry said.

Ginger shook her head. "Huck told me that we're meeting at the Hideout *today*—at four o'clock."

"Nobody told me that! I'm not ready!"
Strawberry exclaimed. "And it's only ten
minutes until four!"

"Well, you'd better hurry!" Ginger said.
"What can I do to help?"

"Um, I need my boots—my black boots!"
Strawberry cried. "And my red skirt . . . and
my pink T-shirt with the star on it!"

The girls scrambled around Strawberry's
house, trying to find all the pieces for her
rock star costume. After several minutes,
they had gathered everything except the
glittery jewelry Strawberry wanted to wear.

"That's okay," Strawberry said
breathlessly as she changed into her
costume. "I bet Blueberry's got awesome
rock-star jewelry I can borrow!"

"Definitely," Ginger said, glancing at the
clock. "Are you ready? We're late!"

"Ready!" Strawberry announced as she put on her hat. "Let's go!"

Meanwhile, Huck was waiting for Ginger to arrive at the Halloween Hideout. "Where is she?" he wondered impatiently. "I've been waiting here forever!" Each time he heard a noise, he ran to the back of the cave to hide. But it was never Ginger.

"I wish I had never thought of this prank," Huck said grumpily. "Ginger probably won't even think my costume is funny. We could have been fixing the roof, but instead I'm wasting my whole day on this dumb prank."

Then Huck heard footsteps approaching! He dashed to the very back of the cave and hid behind a large rock.

"Hello! Hello! We're here!" Ginger called as she ran into the cave.

"Sorry we're late!" added Strawberry.

"Where is everybody?" Ginger asked.

"I don't know," Strawberry replied. "*Somebody* must have been here. The lights are on. *Helloooooo*—is anybody there?"

Suddenly, the lanterns flickered— and all the lights went out! The cave was plunged into darkness.

"St-Strawberry?" Ginger asked. "Wh-what happened?"

"The batteries must have run out," Strawberry said. "Don't worry. There's a flashlight and extra batteries at the back of the cave. Hold my hand. We'll go get them together."

Slowly, the girls crept toward the back of the cave. Then Ginger stopped suddenly.

"Strawberry! Did you hear that?"

"Hear what?" Strawberry whispered.

"It sounded like—like footsteps!" Ginger replied. "I don't want to go any farther. I think we should get out of here!"

"But Ginger, we need the flashlight to find the extra batteries and fix the lanterns," Strawberry said. "I didn't hear any footsteps except our own. Come on; you won't be scared once we get the lights on."

"Okay," Ginger finally said. She glanced around nervously and took a few steps forward.

And then it happened: A glowing skeleton appeared at the back of the cave!

"AHHHHH!" Ginger screamed. She dropped Strawberry's hand and ran out of the cave—leaving Strawberry behind!

Chapter 5

"Wait! Stop! It's only me!" a boy's muffled voice called.

Strawberry's heart was pounding. "Huck?" she asked. "Is that you?"

Huck turned on the flashlight and pulled off his mask. "Yeah, it's me," he said sheepishly. "What are you doing here? Where's Ginger?"

Strawberry was confused. "I'm here to make costumes. What are *you* doing? Why were you hiding in the back of the cave?"

Huck looked down and shuffled his feet. He sighed.

"Well?" Strawberry asked. "What's going on?"

"I was just playing a little prank," Huck admitted. "See, Ginger said she was afraid of skeletons—"

"So you dressed up like one to scare her?" Strawberry exclaimed. "What were you thinking? Poor Ginger!" She turned around and ran out of the cave. "Ginger! Where are you? Everything's okay!"

It wasn't hard to find Ginger Snap. She was pacing outside, trying not to cry.

"Strawberry! I'm so sorry I left you in the cave with that—that—that *thing*!" Ginger cried. "Are you okay? I feel awful!"

"No, Ginger, don't worry about it,"

Strawberry said. "I'm fine." She turned back and called into the cave. "Why don't you come out?"

"What are you doing?" gasped Ginger. Her eyes grew wide as Huck slowly walked out of the cave. "Huck? What are you—why are you—what's going on?"

"Ginger, I was just trying to play a funny prank," Huck said miserably. "I thought you'd know it was me and get a good laugh out of a dancing skeleton. But then the batteries burned out in the lanterns, and it was so dark, and—"

Ginger's eyes flashed angrily. "You mean you dressed up as a skeleton to scare me?" she yelled. "Shame on you, Huck! I told you I was afraid because I trusted you. And all you wanted to do was play a mean trick on me. Well, guess what? I don't want to hang out with you, or talk to you, or see you. I don't want to be your friend anymore."

"No—I—" Huck began.

But Ginger put her hand in the air. "I will *never* forgive you, Huckleberry Pie." She turned around and stormed away.

Huck sat on the ground and buried his head in his hands. "This is awful!" he said. "Now Ginger will never be my friend again, and *you're* mad at me, Strawberry, and everybody else will be, too!"

"I'm not mad at you, Huck," Strawberry said gently as she sat next to him. "I don't think your prank was a berry good idea. And you definitely owe Ginger an apology. But I know you didn't mean to upset her."

"I didn't! Honest!" Huck exclaimed. "What should I do?"

"You know what to do, Huck," replied

Strawberry. "You have to make things right with Ginger—whatever it takes."

Huck nodded. "Okay. I'll see you here tomorrow—when everyone meets to make costumes."

"Right," Strawberry said. "Just give Ginger some time to cool off. After you apologize, things will be back to normal. See you tomorrow!"

The next afternoon, Strawberry put on her rock star costume again and went to the Halloween Hideout. She made sure to get there early so that she could replace the batteries in the lanterns before her friends arrived.

One by one, the other members of the Friendship Club walked into the cave.

Most of them were wearing parts of their costumes.

"Angel, you look berry pretty!" Strawberry exclaimed as Angel showed off her pink-and-purple ball gown.

"Why, thank you, Miss Strawberry." Angel giggled. "All I need now is jewelry and hair ribbons. Blueberry, are you a detective? Berry cool!"

Blueberry grinned. "That's Sherlock Muffin to you," she teased as she peered through a magnifying glass. "Huck, where's your costume?"

Huck looked at the ground. "I don't have one yet," he said. "I was gonna be a skeleton, but I want to come up with a different idea."

"Well, you're in luck!" Blueberry announced as she opened a trunk of costumes.

"Hey—wait a minute. Where's Ginger?" asked Orange. "Shouldn't we wait for her?"

"Oh, I don't want to wait a minute longer!" Angel said impatiently. She grabbed her cell phone. "I'm going to call her and see what's taking so long."

Strawberry and Huck exchanged a worried look as Angel dialed Ginger's number.

"Hello, Ginger? Where are you?" Angel said into the phone. "We're all waiting for you at the Halloween Hideout and—what? He *what*? And you're—but—Ginger! Really?" Angel sighed. "Okay, I'll tell them. Wait—Ginger—what about fixing the roof? Oh. Okay. Bye."

Angel hung up the phone and turned back to the group. "Ginger isn't coming. She said that Huck played a mean trick on her yesterday and she's not going to hang out with him ever again—or with *us* when Huck is around! *And* she won't work on the roof with Huck anymore."

"Huck, what did you do?" asked Orange.

"It was just a stupid prank!" Huck exclaimed. "I didn't know it was going to make Ginger so mad! I went to her house to apologize this morning, but she slammed the door in my face!"

"Well, that's just great. Now Halloween is going to be ruined!" Angel said loudly. "It won't be nearly as much fun if Ginger isn't here! And what about the clubhouse? If only one of you works on the roof, we'll be lucky if it's fixed before winter comes."

"This is all my fault," Huck said miserably. "I'll skip Halloween. Then you

guys can hang out with
Ginger, and I'll fix as much of
the roof as I can."

"But Huck, Halloween won't be
nearly as much fun without *you*, either,"
Strawberry said. "And honestly, Angel is
right. The roof will never get fixed with
only one person working on it. Won't you
try talking to Ginger again? Please?"

"Sure," Huck said. "I'll go to her house
now. But I don't know what good it will do."
Huck turned and walked out of the cave.

Strawberry sighed. "I'm sure that Ginger
will forgive Huck . . . eventually," she said.
"But until she does, let's stop making
Halloween plans. Okay?"

"Okay," agreed the rest of her friends.

And sadly, quietly, they all trudged out
of the cave and headed home.

Chapter 6

The next morning, Strawberry called Huck. "Hi, Huck!" she said cheerfully. "How's everything?"

"Not good." Huck sighed. "I *tried* to talk to Ginger again. But she wouldn't listen to me. I don't know how I can convince her that I'm sorry."

"I don't like it when my friends are upset with each other," Strawberry said. "It's not berry friendly at all. Maybe I'll try talking to Ginger."

"Really?" Huck said hopefully. "Thanks, Strawberry! If anyone can make her understand, *you* can."

"I can't make any promises," Strawberry warned. "But I'll do my berry best."

"Can you stop by before you go to Ginger's house?" asked Huck. "I made something for her."

"Are you sure you don't want to give it to her yourself?" Strawberry said.

"It's probably better if you take it to her," Huck replied. "Besides, I've got to get over to the clubhouse and work on the roof."

"Okay, Huck," Strawberry said. "See you soon. Bye!"

Strawberry hung up the phone, but a minute later she picked it back up to call

Blueberry, Orange, and Angel. She had a feeling she was going to need a little help when she talked to Ginger—and who better to help than the rest of the Friendship Club?

An hour later, the girls walked to Ginger's house. Ginger was outside raking leaves.

"Hi, guys!" Ginger said. "What are you doing here? Strawberry, what's in that box?"

"Oh, we can talk about that later," Strawberry said as she put a large box on the ground. "But first we want to talk about Huck."

The smile faded from Ginger's face.

"Well, I *don't* want to talk about Huck," she replied. "I don't even want to hear his name."

"Really, Ginger?" asked Strawberry. "I'm surprised. I never thought you were the kind of person to hold a grudge."

"I'm not!" protested Ginger. "I don't hold grudges."

"What would you call it when someone won't forgive a friend who made a mistake? Even when they've apologized again and again?" asked Blueberry.

Ginger stared at the ground. She didn't say anything.

"When you stopped being friends with Huck, it affected the whole Friendship Club," Strawberry said. "No one's had any fun with both of you missing."

"What about the clubhouse roof? How

will that ever get fixed without your help?" added Angel.

Orange smiled kindly at Ginger. "Come on, Ginger, fighting is no fun! Don't you want to get back to the important stuff, like fixing the roof and getting ready for Halloween?"

"Well, yeah!" said Ginger. "But I'm still too mad at Huck to be friends with him."

"Remember when Angel got mad at you for scaring her with that story?" Strawberry asked. "If she hadn't forgiven you, no one would have had fun at the sleepover—and you would be missing her friendship. Just like you'll miss being friends with Huck if you can't find a way to forgive him. Just . . . think about it, okay?"

"Okay," Ginger replied in a quiet voice.

"This is from Huck," Strawberry said,

pushing the box over to Ginger. "He's working on the clubhouse roof today, if you want to talk to him. I hope you will. See you later, Ginger."

After her friends left, Ginger opened the box to find glass vials filled with white powder, beakers filled with clear liquid, and little bottles of different colored liquids. "What *is* this?" she wondered. She read the note inside the box.

Hi, Ginger,

Here are some props you can use when you wear your Halloween costume. Just combine the baking soda, vinegar, and food coloring in the beakers and you'll have a really cool mad scientist experiment!

Since I probably won't see you, I hope you have an awesome Halloween. I'm really sorry about that stupid prank. I thought it might help you get over your fear. I would never, ever have done it if I'd thought it would scare you so badly or if I'd known that it would make you stop being my friend.

Huck

Ginger sighed as she folded the note. Maybe her friends were right. Maybe Huck really was sorry. The only way to find out would be to talk to him. So Ginger set off for the clubhouse.

Ginger found Huck on a ladder, trying to drag some boards up to the roof. He was only holding onto the ladder with one hand, and his hat was falling into his eyes!

"Huck! What are you doing?" Ginger cried, forgetting that she was mad. "That's not safe!" She ran over and held the boards so that Huck could climb the ladder and then pull them onto the roof.

"You're right," Huck said. "But I didn't know how else to get the boards up here."

"Fixing the roof is a two-person job," Ginger said. She started climbing the ladder. "If you can't do a job safely by yourself, you shouldn't do it at all."

"I know, but how else was the roof going to get fixed?" Huck sighed. "Hey. What are you doing here? I thought you never wanted to see me again."

Ginger sighed. "I'm sorry, Huck. That

was a mean thing to say. I was just so mad!"

"Yeah, I know," Huck said. "But I don't blame you. I would have been mad, too, if someone had done that to me. I'm really sorry."

"Thanks, Huck," Ginger replied. "And thanks for the mad scientist experiment! I can't wait to try it out!"

"No problem," Huck said. "Now I just have to figure out what I'm going to be for Halloween. I'm not wearing that skeleton costume ever again!"

Ginger's dark eyes twinkled. "After we get some work done on the roof, we can work on your costume!" she suggested.

"Good—because I need all the help I can get!" Huck grinned.

Over the next several days, the Friendship Club was busier than ever as the kids worked on the clubhouse and finished getting ready for Halloween. The day before Halloween, the roof was finally fixed!

"This is amazing!" Strawberry exclaimed. "I can't believe you finished already!"

"I couldn't have done it without Ginger," Huck said.

"And *I* couldn't have done it without Huck!" replied Ginger.

"The clubhouse will be back to normal soon," Angel said.

"Which means it will be time to say good-bye to the Halloween Hideout," Strawberry said. "I think we should have a

Halloween party there!"

"Yeah!" cheered Huck. "We can play games and eat candy before we go trick-or-treating!"

"Let's all bring one game and one Halloween treat to share," suggested Blueberry.

"Good idea," Strawberry said. "I can hardly wait!"

On Halloween, Strawberry dressed up in her rock star costume, complete with pink hair extensions and jewelry borrowed from Blueberry. The sun was starting to set as she hurried to the Halloween Hideout. Inside the cave, the walls were decorated with orange and black streamers and

balloons. The lanterns glowed warmly, and hanging bats and ghosts cast spooky shadows on the walls. The rest of the Friendship Club was waiting for her.

"Happy Halloween, Strawberry!" everyone exclaimed.

"Happy Halloween!" replied Strawberry. "The Hideout looks awesome—and so do all of you! Your costumes are amazing!"

"So is yours!" said Orange, who was dressed as a vampire. "Would you like some blood punch to drink?"

"And a vanilla ghost cupcake?" added Angel.

"Sure!" Strawberry giggled as she sipped Orange's fruit punch. "Yummy!"

"What's that?" asked Angel, pointing at the vials and beakers Huck had given Ginger.

"My greatest experiment—watch this!"

cried Ginger. She put on her goggles and poured baking soda into a beaker of purple vinegar, and the mixture bubbled and fizzed.

"Awesome!" Strawberry said. "I'm berry impressed!"

"I couldn't have done it without my loyal assistant Igor." Ginger grinned at Huck, who hunched his back and made a funny face.

"Igor want candy!" Huck yelled. "Lots of candy!"

"Time for a game! My game is a haunted treasure hunt," Detective Blueberry said. "If you solve all the clues, you *might* find lots of berry special Halloween treats!"

"Lots of treats!" Huck said in Igor's voice.

"And no more tricks," Strawberry said happily. "I *knew* this was going to be the berry best Halloween ever!"